To all the MOMMIES who make the world a
better place with their kindness, talents, and
love for their families.

For Hazel, Lola, and Daniel:
You are my sunshine, always.

Love, Mommy

What are MOMMIES made of?
While sugar and spice
seem very nice,
they are best served
in a pie slice.

This is not to say
MOMMIES aren't sweet.
A hug from a MOMMY
is a one-of-a-kind treat.

MOMMIES are very
special people, indeed.
They are unique and thoughtful,
caring for every need.

Whether you're hungry,
tired, or you want to play,
a MOMMY knows how
to make your day.

With a fun game, a big kiss,
or yummy food,
MOMMY can put you
in a good mood.

However, there's more to MOMMIES
that I'm sure you know.

The many things they can do
and teach, to help you grow.

MOMMIES can be strong
with a loud voice to speak.

They can be outgoing
or have a quiet streak.

Even if MOMMY is shy
or likes to bake,
she might also shoot hoops
and fish on a lake.

A MOMMY can play sports
like tennis or soccer,
or she might be a runner,
yogi, or walker.

MOMMIES love science,
tech, writing, and art.
She'll show you activities
that are close to her heart.

MOMMIES can work in the office or from home.

She can even work outside where the animals roam.

Whether she works all day
or for just a few hours,
when she's done, you'll play
blocks, building towers.

Some MOMMIES are creative,
while others are good at math.
She'll share her talents while
you play in the bath.

A MOMMY can make up
a silly dance or a song,
in hopes that you'll boogie
and sing along.

While a **MOMMY** is
clever, goofy, and fun,
sometimes she'll be tough
on you, her little one.

It's not because she's mad
at you, or being mean,
MOMMIES protect you,
and keep you safe and clean.

On days when MOMMY
is busy or blowing off steam,
there will be a loved one who
cares, your dream team.

Whether you have a
MOMMY or daddy,
or any combo of two,
families work together
because they love you.

MOMMIES can come in any
shape, color, and height.
Her strong arms play catch
or piano, and snuggle at night.

MOMMIES are beautiful, smart,
generous, and kind.
Her qualities will guide you
to make up your own mind.

MOMMIES are all different
in one way or another,
but what's great about MOMMIES:
They support each other.

That's what MOMMIES
are made of.

About the Illustrator

Jennifer Bouron is a French print designer who studied fashion and print design in the west of France. After three years designing in the kids fashion space, Jennifer developed her freelance business, and is known for her contemporary portraits, fashionable illustrations, and striking color choices.

About the Designer

Romy Collective is a Los Angeles based design studio founded by Michelle Brutto in 2016. Brutto has a BFA from Auburn University in graphic design. She creates a unique visual identity for each of her clients, providing a one-of-a-kind design experience and highly polished finished product. She and her husband have two kids.

About the Author

Christa Fletcher grew up in Northern California where she wrote short stories and helped care for her younger brothers. She studied English and Rhetoric at UC Berkeley where she met her husband Daniel. They moved to New York City where she earned her Master's in journalism. She now enjoys playing unicorns and crafting with their daughters in Southern California, and continues to write professionally.

CPSIA information can be obtained
at www.ICGtesting.com
Printed in the USA
BVHW021247310819
557201BV00001B/1/P